The Grand Kokolorum was immensely proud of his new couch. Made of the softest lavender leather, creamy and smooth as butter, it sat softly glowing in an inner chamber of his private quarters. He looked forward to napping on it in the late afternoons, being cradled by its deep cushions, dreaming dreams that would help him govern the land with majesty and decorum.

The Couch of the Grand Kokolorum

Meg Barnhouse

DEDICATION

This book is dedicated to the Karma Fairy's chaos cats, and to all of you who will now be able to say, "Oh yes, Henry. There you are." Also to the Unitarian Universalist children, who are good at learning and who will one day be in charge of quite a lot. And to Kiya, who helps me dream, then makes those dreams come true.

ACKNOWLEDGMENTS

Thanks to George Denny and to Kiya for their encouragement, and to my dad, who always wanted me to write a children's book.

Everyone in the land did as the Grand Kokolorum commanded. His staff scurried from room to room filing his papers, serving him snacks, cleaning up his messes and laughing at his jokes. His people crowded around the windows of the palace trying to catch a glimpse of him.

The only one in the palace who didn't do exactly as commanded was Henry, the Grand Kokolorum's large yellow cat. He was used to sleeping on the old couch, so he jumped right up onto the soft new lavender leather, closed his eyes and went to sleep.

"NO! No, no no no, Henry!" shouted the Grand Kokolorum. "You are not to sleep on this couch. You have your own spot in the corner of the rug and you are to sleep there. We will keep this new couch simply perfect with no yellow hair and no claw marks."
The Grand Kokolorum explained the new rules to Henry several times, but when he came into the inner chamber after a hard day at work he would find Henry asleep on the new couch. Hearing the Grand Kokolorum come in, Henry would open one yellow eye, give him a long look, and close it again.

The Grand Kokolorum got jumping mad, fist-clenching mad. When he jumped up and down, the decorations on his hat and the long toes of his shoes jiggled crazily. "I am the Grand Kokolorum!" he shouted. "You have to do as I say, Henry!" Henry's whiskers twitched as he slowly descended from the smooth lavender cushions.

He decided to teach Henry a lesson. Setting mouse traps on the cushions, he said to himself "So there! Henry will get a big pinch and then he won't hop up there anymore, and I'll be able to keep my couch simply perfect!"
While he was in the throne room at work, Henry swiped at the mousetraps with his paw, knocking them to the floor, where they snapped shut on empty air.

After work, there Henry was, sleeping on the couch, mousetraps all over the floor, regarding the Grand Kokolorum with dreamy yellow eyes, full of the thoughts that came from being cradled in soft leather.

The Grand Kokolorum shrieked for a servant to come gather up the mousetraps and then he ordered some big metal traps with sharp teeth. Trembling, the servant set the cruel traps on the soft leather couch. Henry watched with glowing eyes.

That afternoon he ran into the inner chamber, hoping the cat had seen the traps and stayed off the couch. One of the big traps lay, sprung, on the floor, and, curled on the cushion where it had sat, was Henry, purring in his sleep.

The Grand Kokolorum snapped. He was the ruler of almost everything, and it was unbearable that he could not be the ruler over this one warm and purring cat. His angry arm swept down toward Henry, springing the second waiting trap, which sunk its teeth into the billowing cloth of the Grand Kokolorum's jacket, causing him to screech like a big bird.

Grabbing a candle from its stand, he set the couch on fire. "Now you will not be able to sleep on my beautiful perfect couch!" he yelled. As the flames devoured the lavender leather, servants rushed in with many pitchers of water and finally put out the fire. The couch was a smoldering ruin, stinking, sticky and gray.

The room filled up with shocked silence. The Grand Kokolorum's head cleared for a moment, as if the fire had broken a spell. "Oh, look, Henry," the Grand Kokolorum cried. "Look what I've done. Our beautiful couch is in ruins." Henry, curled up on the floor, looked at him with a wise yellow gaze. "I thought that, since I was the ruler of quite a lot, I could rule over absolutely everything. What a silly mistake." Exhausted from all of his screaming and jumping around, he lay his head down on his pillowy purring cat and closed his eyes. The Grand Kokolorum finally slept, and dreamt dreams that would help him govern his land with majesty and decorum.

The End

ABOUT THE AUTHOR

Meg Barnhouse is the Grand Koko --- er --- the minister of the First Unitarian Universalist Church of Austin, Texas. She is the mother of two wise, funny and handsome sons, the delighted mother-in-law of a woman she adores, and the partner of Kiya Heartwood, a singer-songwriter and composer. They have two cats, four chickens, a worm bin and a dog, and they are rich in friends and family. Meg is the author of six other books. She has three CDs. Two are CDs of her original songs, and one is an audio version of some of her best-loved stories.

For more about Meg please visit:

www.megbarnhouse.com.

Proof

Made in the USA
Charleston, SC
10 November 2011